Akbar's Dream

Written by Jane Langford
Illustrated by Joanne Moss

Heinemann

Chapter 1

Akbar had a dream. His dream was to make the most beautiful silk cloth in the whole of India.

It was the summer holidays. Every day, Akbar sat with his grandfather at the loom. They wove long lengths of silk with the most wonderful patterns. 'Look at the pattern I have just made,' said Akbar.

Grandfather looked at the piece of silk.

'It is very good!' he said.

'Thank you, Grandfather,' said Akbar. 'One day soon, I will make the most beautiful silk cloth in the whole of India.'

Grandfather smiled and shook his head. 'That is impossible,' he said.

'Why?' asked Akbar.

'Because you are only a young boy. You are only eight years old.'

'That doesn't matter!' said Akbar.

Akbar was annoyed. It did not matter how old he was. He knew he could make the most beautiful silk cloth in India. It was his dream.

Grandfather thought for a moment.

'We must go to Agra to see the Taj Mahal,' he said. 'It is the most beautiful building in India. Perhaps you will see some patterns there that will help you to make the most beautiful silk cloth in India.'

Akbar was pleased. Grandfather often told him about the Taj Mahal. The great emperor, Shah Jahan, had ordered twenty thousand craftsmen to build the Taj Mahal. Its white marble walls were covered with jewels.

'Can we really go to see the Taj Mahal?' asked Akbar.

Every year, Grandfather talked about going to see the Taj Mahal. Every year, he was either too busy to go, or he did not have enough money for the train fare.

'Yes,' said Grandfather. 'I have saved nearly enough rupees for the train fare. If we sell the silk cloth that you have just made, we will have enough money.'

Grandfather and Akbar folded up the silk and took it through the streets to the market. Soon they reached Omar's stall. Omar was Akbar's uncle. His stall was piled high with bundles of silk cloth.

'Hello, Omar,' said Grandfather.

'Hello,' said Omar. 'What have you got for me today?'

'It's a beautiful piece of silk cloth that Akbar has made,' said Grandfather.

Omar held up the silk cloth and looked at it. He winked at Akbar.

'It is a beautiful silk cloth,' he said, 'but it isn't the most beautiful in India. Look! It is not as beautiful as this one!' Omar pointed to a roll of red and gold silk cloth that would be used for a wedding sari.

Akbar smiled. He knew that his uncle was teasing him. Everyone knew about his dream. Everyone knew that he wanted to make the most beautiful silk cloth in India.

'I am going to see the Taj Mahal,' said Akbar, 'and when I come back I will make the most beautiful silk cloth in India.'

'Is this true?' asked Omar. 'Are you really going to see the Taj Mahal?'

'Yes,' said Grandfather. 'If you will give us a good price for Akbar's silk, we will go tomorrow.'

Tomorrow! Akbar had not dreamed that it would be so soon!

'Will you buy my silk, Uncle Omar?' he begged. 'I must go with Grandfather to see the Taj Mahal.'

Uncle Omar smiled. He counted out some money and gave it to Grandfather. 'Now will you have enough for the train tickets?' he asked.

Grandfather counted the money. Uncle Omar had been very kind.

'I will indeed!' he said. 'Tomorrow we will go to see the Taj Mahal. Run home, Akbar, and tell your father.'

Akbar ran home as fast as he could. He had a lot to do before tomorrow. He had to find paper on which to draw new patterns, and pencils to mark the colours. When he saw the Taj Mahal, he was going to make the most beautiful silk cloth in India.

Chapter 2

The train journey to Agra was a long one. Akbar sat in his seat and looked out of the window.

'I can't wait to see the Taj Mahal,' he said. 'Are we nearly there?'

'Not quite yet,' said Grandfather. 'Shall I tell you a story to help pass the time?'

'Yes, please, Grandfather,' said Akbar. 'Tell me the story of the Taj Mahal.'

Grandfather smiled. He sat back in his seat and began.

'A long time ago, a young prince met a beautiful girl. She had a market stall close to the palace. The prince wanted to buy all the goods from her stall, but she would not let him. She smiled at him and made him laugh. The prince, Shah Jahan, fell in love with her.'

After several years they got
married. Shah Jahan became
Emperor. He called his wife Mumtaz
Mahal, which meant "Chosen one of
the Palace". He loved her very much
and she was never very far from
his side.

One day, Shah Jahan had to go
and fight a battle. While he and his
soldiers were away fighting, Mumtaz
gave birth to a little girl. The baby
survived, but sadly Mumtaz died.

Grandfather stopped speaking. There were tears in his eyes. Akbar did not know if the tears were for Mumtaz or for Grandma. Grandma had died last year and Grandfather was still very lonely.

'Did you love Grandma as much as Shah Jahan loved Mumtaz?' asked Akbar.

Grandfather nodded. 'I did,' he said. 'But I am not sad. Grandma and I had a long and happy life together.'

'Was Shah Jahan sad?' asked Akbar.

'He was very sad,' said
Grandfather. 'Everyone in the
country was sad too. No one was
allowed to dance or laugh, or sing.
Shah Jahan did not want his wife to
be forgotten. He sent for craftsmen
from all over India and ordered them
to build the finest tomb in the whole
world. It took them twenty years to
build the Taj Mahal.'

Akbar stared out of the carriage
window. Twenty years was a very
long time.

'Grandfather,' he said, 'I don't want to take twenty years to make the most beautiful silk cloth in India. I want to make it now.'

Grandfather nodded his head wisely. 'I know you do,' he said, 'but first you must have a plan. You must know what you want the silk to look like. You must know its colour and its pattern. Do you know those things already?'

'No,' said Akbar, 'not really. I have ideas. I have pictures in my mind, but they are not very clear. When I try to draw the pattern of what I see, it disappears from my head.'

'That happens to me too,' said Grandfather. 'Now I only make the patterns that I know well. I make the patterns that my father made, and his father before him.'

'I want to make new patterns,' said Akbar. 'I want to make patterns that no one has ever seen on silk before.'

'You are like Shah Jahan,' said Grandfather. 'You want to make the most beautiful thing that has ever been seen.'

This was true. Akbar knew that he would never be happy until he had made the silk he dreamed of. He hoped that the Taj Mahal would fill him with ideas for the silk's pattern and its colours. As soon as he knew what they were, he could start work.

19

'Look!' said Grandfather. 'We are in Agra. We can't be far from the Taj Mahal now.'

The train stopped and many people got out. Grandfather and Akbar let themselves be carried along the platform by the crowds. Soon they were in the streets, heading for the Taj Mahal.

'I can see it!' cried Akbar.

A beautiful white dome sparkled in the sunlight and four tall towers stretched into the sky.

'Isn't it wonderful?' gasped Grandfather.

Akbar didn't answer. He was too busy gazing at the Taj Mahal. Even in his dreams, he had not imagined anything quite so lovely.

Chapter 3

As soon as Akbar saw the Taj Mahal, he knew that this was the best moment of his life.

The gardens of the Taj Mahal stretched in front of him. Akbar's eyes went past the canals and the green trees to the very end of the gardens. There stood the Taj Mahal.

Akbar walked slowly towards it with Grandfather.

23

The closer he got, the more clearly he could see the jewels set into the marble walls. They were red, green and yellow. They made patterns of roses and tulips.

'This is the pattern I want,' gasped Akbar. 'This is the pattern for my silk cloth.'

'Wait,' said Grandfather. 'There is more inside.'

'It can't be more beautiful than this!' said Akbar. He got out his paper and pencils, then started to sketch the patterns that he could see.

He drew flowers and leaves, twisting and twirling and curling together. He chose colours that he had never used before. They were the colours of the shining jewels. Akbar drew and drew until his hand hurt.

'That is enough, Akbar,' said Grandfather, gently. 'Let us go inside now.'

Akbar followed Grandfather into the building. Inside was Mumtaz's tomb. It stood on a high platform. Next to it stood another tomb.

'Whose tomb is that?' asked Akbar.

'It belongs to Shah Jahan,' whispered Grandfather. 'He asked to be buried next to his wife.'

Round the two tombs stood a marble screen. It was carved to look like lace and decorated with rubies and emeralds. The twisting, turning flowers that covered the screen were even more beautiful than the ones Akbar had seen outside.

'Are you going to copy these flowers?' asked Grandfather.

Akbar shook his head. 'No,' he said. 'My sketches could never show the beauty of these flowers.'

When Akbar had seen enough of the tombs, they went back outside.

Akbar's mind was swirling with colours and ideas and patterns.

'I want to go home,' he said.

Grandfather and Akbar took the train back home. They travelled together in silence. They were both lost in their dreams. Grandfather dreamed of Grandma and how she would have loved to see the Taj Mahal. Akbar dreamed of the silk cloth he was going to weave.

When they got home, Akbar sat down by the loom. He looked at the coloured threads he had and realised that he would need new colours for his silk cloth.

'Can we go and see Uncle Omar tomorrow?' he asked.

Grandfather took Akbar to
Omar's stall. They chose new colours
of silk thread for Akbar to weave.

'The green must be like
emeralds,' said Akbar, 'and the red
must be like rubies.'

Omar found the colours that
Akbar wanted.

'I don't want any money for the
thread,' said Omar. 'I just want to see
the finished silk cloth.'

Akbar took the thread home and started work. He looked at the sketches he had made. He shut his eyes and thought about the patterns that swirled round in his head. He thought of the tulips and the roses. He thought about the towers and the dome.

Little by little, Akbar wove his design. The ideas that were trapped inside his head, became trapped in the pattern of the silk.

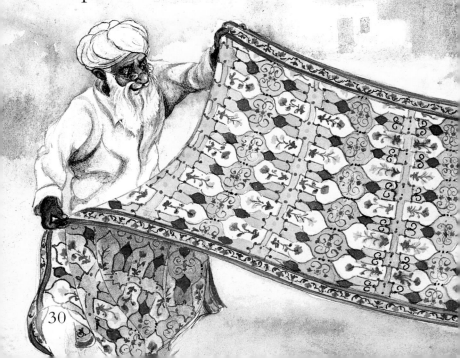

The cloth grew longer and longer. It grew more and more beautiful. At last Akbar had finished it. He held it up for everyone to see.

'It's beautiful!' gasped Grandfather in amazement.

'I've done what I said I would, Grandfather. I have made the most beautiful silk cloth in the whole of India!'

'Let's take it to show Uncle Omar!' said Grandfather. 'He will want to see it!'

Grandfather and Akbar hurried through the streets. They found Omar at his stall.

'Look, Uncle Omar!' said Akbar. 'Look at what I have made!'

Uncle Omar could not believe his eyes. He took the silk from Akbar and cradled it in his arms. He brushed his fingers tenderly over the cloth. He gazed at the wonderful patterns. Finally, he let out a soft sigh.

'Akbar,' he said, 'this is truly the most beautiful silk cloth in India! One day it will be as famous as the Taj Mahal and you will be as famous as Shah Jahan!'